Miles Away In
The Caribbean

BY YOLANDA T. MARSHALL
Illustrated by Beatriz Mello

First Printing, 2019

ISBN: 9781999115500

Garnalma Press

It's story time, my little ones; I have an exciting book.
Gather around, and let's have a look.
It's about a boy named Miles who travels in a magical spaceship.
He visited beautiful countries while on his Caribbean trip.

Hello, Antigua and Barbuda!
I can see your highest mountain top.
Let's make a stop on Mount Obama.
Wow! There are hundreds of beaches here,
so many I can see.
Is that my tummy grumbling? Yep! Time to eat delicious fungee!

Here I am, in the Bahamas,
diving in the world's deepest water-filled sinkhole,
Dean's Blue Hole.
Under the noon day's sun, I go bonefishing.
In the warm tropical waters, you will find me relaxing.

Greetings, Barbados!
I am here to explore Harrison's Cave, with lots of
limestone formations to admire,
and flowing streams of crystal-clear water.
There are Grandpa and Mama Cathy,
with my favourite Bajan dish.
Cheese on bread! It's cou-cou and flying fish!

Good morning, Belize!
What a beautiful day to feel the island's breeze
blowing the sweet, earthy scent from the cacao trees,
which are used to make chocolate bars. Oh, so yummy!
Yikes! The pumas, jaguars, and crocodiles are chasing me!

Bonjour, Dominica!
A heated adventure awaits.
The steam is rising from the Boiling Lake.
In my spaceship I'll remain, don't want to burn my little toes
while flying high over the magnificent volcanoes.

I am in Grenada,
known as the island of spice!
I smell nutmeg, cloves, saffron, cinnamon, and everything nice.
Mmmmm like Mommy's kitchen,
when she sings sweet calypso while baking.

Dear Guyana,
on the continent of South America, the land of many waters.
I'll fly over the lush rainforest, the Kaieteur Falls, and Mount Roraima,
and share smiles with the diverse faces welcoming me.
We'll sing together, *"Your children salute you, dear land of the free."*

Bonjour Haiti,
Sak pasè? It's a Rara parade! Time to dance,
in a colourful costume for my vibrant performance.
Bring the bamboo trumpets, maracas, and the drums.
Celebrating all day, until sundown.

Jamaica, mi deh yah!
Time to splash in the water of the Dunn's River Falls.
I made new friends while playing dandy shandy, soccer, and netball.
Driving through Kingston, I visited Trench Town,
where I enjoyed skanking to reggae songs.

Montserrat, are you ready?
I joined the Masquerade Troupes,
with a painted mask and a tall hat, and I pranced along with this group.
This emerald island came alive, as the crowd wore green to sing and play,
I am celebrating St Patrick's Day.

It's a sunny day in Saint Kitts and Nevis!
Oh wow, what a view! On top of Timothy Hill, along the coastline,
I can see the Brimstone Hill Fortress; history preserved under the
sunshine.
"Hey, where's my mango?" a tourist yells as she searches around frantically.
I chuckled and pointed out the culprit; a cute, yet mischievous monkey.

Sa ka fèt, Saint Lucia!
I got lost in the hustle and bustle of Castries Market.
Vendors sold guava, passion fruit, coconut, and little trinkets.
There is a special place I had to visit while here;
the library located in Derek Walcott Square.

Saint Vincent and the Grenadines, what a lovely day
to play at the beach with black sand between my toes
and visit the city of arches, walk on cobblestones,
dive with the whales, dolphins, and manatees, and
whistle with the warblers as they fly from tree to tree.

Good morning, Suriname!
What's brewing in the Witch's Market? I'll peek
at the hidden potions and tempting Dutch treats.
Miss De Vries is serving Pom! YUM! I won't turn down this offer
to have a taste of Suriname's blended cultures.

Trinidad and Tobago, let's play mas!
I hear the joyful laughter of the carnival crowd
blowing their horns and whistles out loud
and singing the lyrics of their favourite soca songs,
as I dance to the beats of the steel pan all day long!

"Where should I visit next? Ah ha! Cuba!"
But, Miles was exhausted after having so much fun on his trip to the Caribbean.
In his magical spaceship, he flew home to Canada, and share stories of his adventures.

Dedicated to my family in Antigua and Barbuda, Bahamas, Barbados, Belize, Dominica, Grenada, Guyana, Haiti, Jamaica, Montserrat, Saint Kitts and Nevis, Saint Lucia, Saint Vincent and the Grenadines, Suriname, Trinidad and Tobago, Anguilla, Bermuda, British Virgin Islands, Cayman Islands, Turks and Caicos Islands, Aruba, Colombia, Curaçao, Dominican Republic, Mexico, Puerto Rico, Sint Maarten, and Venezuela.

CPSIA information can be obtained
at www.ICGtesting.com
Printed in the USA
LVHW071515141219
640499LV00021B/398/P